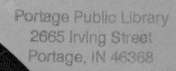

A great big hug to my wife, Denise,
and our boys, Chase and Zane
—C.C.

To Daisy and Casey, my angels
—J.M.

www.randomhouse.com/kids

Library of congress cataloging-in-Publication Data
crandall, court.
Hugville / by court crandall ; illustrations by Joe Murray. — 1st ed.
p. cm.
SUMMARY: The mayor of Hugville conducts a tour of the town where all kinds of hugs are practiced and celebrated, including the monkey hug, tornado hug, and phone hug.
ISBN 0-375-82418-9 (trade) — ISBN 0-375-92418-3 (lib. bdg.)
[1. Hugging—Fiction. 2. Stories in rhyme.] I. Murray, Joe, ill. II. Title.
PZ8.3.C84475Hu 2005
[E]—dc21
2002153362

PRINTED IN MALAYSIA   First Edition   10 9 8 7 6 5 4 3 2 1
RANDOM HOUSE and colophon are registered trademarks of Random House, Inc.

Hugville

by Court Crandall

illustrated by Joe Murray

Random House New York

I'm so happy to see you, my dear little friend!
As Lord Mayor of Hugville, I'd like to extend
A great big warm welcome to cross the town line
And sample each hug on the Hugville town sign.

WELCOME
to
HUGVILLE

POPULATION:
25,000 HUGS

• Monkey Hug • Octopus Hug •
Tornado Hug • Itchy Dog Hug •
Phone Hug • Pogo Hug •
Stick Hug • Chicken Hug •

The first stop on our tour is the Hugville Grade School,
Where kids learn to hug from the time they can drool.

It takes exactly **6,423** hug credits to graduate from Hugville Grade School.

There's hug science, hug math—even hug history.
Each taught by someone with a hug P.H.D.*

*Professional Hugging Degree

The Monkey Hug's one that every child knows.
Climb up a friend's limbs all the way to his nose.
Scratch under your arms like you've seen monkeys do.
Then end your hug hooting, "Eee! Eee!" and "Ooh! Ooh!"

While doing the Monkey Hug, it's also acceptable to pick bugs off each other.

HUGVILLE TOWN ZOO

It can take hours to untangle an Octopus Hug.

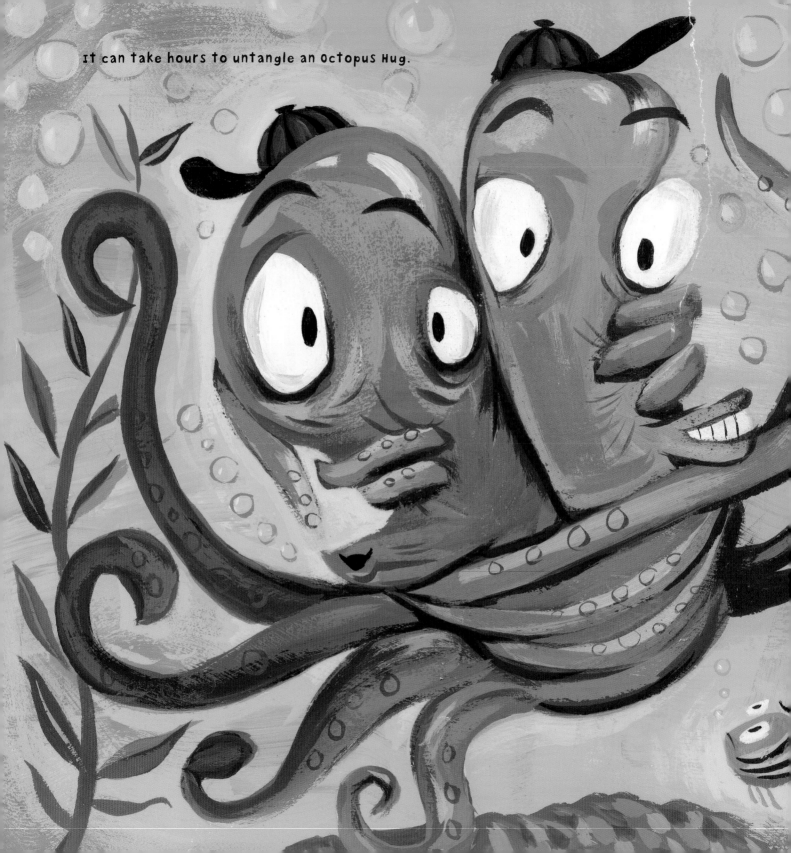

The Octopus Hug's where you wrap someone up,
As if each of your toes had its own suction cup.
Take all of your limbs, multiply them by two,
And pretend you are hugging down in the deep blue.

In Hugville you'll find if you've got a sore head,
The Hug Doctor prescribes two hugs before bed.
Come morning you'll see you are back on your feet
And ready to hug every person you meet.

With the Tornado Hug, you will spin 'round and 'round—
As if a hug twister has blown into town.
Just hold your pal tight and twirl through the room.
Then follow your hug with a dustpan and broom.

Warning: Too much Tornado Hugging can lead to a bad hair day.

The Itchy Dog Hug's like a canine with fleas,
All over his skin from his head to his knees.
The way that it works is you scratch, then you rub,
Like two mangy mutts in sore need of a tub.

In Hugville, this hug lasts sixty seconds.

That's seven minutes in dog years.

The Phone Hug's for huggers who live far away.
It's not what you do, but more what you say.
Just pick up the phone and call someone who's dear
And pass her a hug from your mouth to her ear.

It's possible to enter a Hugvillian phone booth as an ordinary hugger and come out . . . a Super Hugger!

PHONE BOOK

The Pogo Stick Hug's where your legs become springs.
It's a hug that has many poing-boings and ping-bings.
First hug on the floor and then jump in the air.
If you hug long enough, well, the neighbors may stare.

If you bounce too high and hit something,
that's called a Sore Head Hug.

The Chicken Hug's one that begins with a cluck.
If you're looking for laughs, it seems you're in luck.
You hug with your wings while you perch on one leg.
But don't squeeze too hard or you might lay an egg!

If you do this hug on a hot day, it's called a *Fried* Chicken Hug.

The Hug Jug is kept in our Hugville Town Square.
And each night at sunset we all gather there.
Please join us by sticking your hand in the pot.
Then pull out a hug and yell which one you've got.

You've hugged across town from one side to the other,
And there's just one hug left to give to another—
Pretend that your arms are all covered with glue
And hug the one reading this story to **you**!

Hogville

The best way to get a glued hugger unstuck is to tickle under his arms.